The Vampire Book

SALLY REGAN

**LONDON, NEW YORK,
MELBOURNE, MUNICH, AND DELHI**

Project editor Jenny Finch
Senior art editor Stefan Podhorodecki
Designers Keith Davis, Johnny Pau, Yumiko Tahata
Editorial assistant Jessamy Wood

Managing editor Linda Esposito
Managing art editor Diane Thistlethwaite
Publishing manager Andrew Macintyre
Category publisher Laura Buller

Creative retouching Steve Willis
Picture research Nic Dean
DK picture library Lucy Claxton
Production editor Maria Elia
Senior production controller Angela Graef
Jacket designer Yumiko Tahata
Jacket editor Mariza O'Keeffe
Design development manager Sophia M Tampakopoulos Turner

Consultant Professor Glennis Byron

First published in Great Britain in 2009 by
Dorling Kindersley Limited,
80 Strand, London, WC2R 0RL

Copyright © 2009 Dorling Kindersley Limited
A Penguin Company

2 4 6 8 10 9 7 5 3 1
175774 – 07/09

A CIP catalogue record for this book
is available from the British Library

ISBN: 978-1-40534-715-0

Design and digital artworking by Stefan Podhorodecki
Hi-res workflow proofed by MDP, UK
Printed and bound by Leo, China

**Discover more at
www.dk.com**

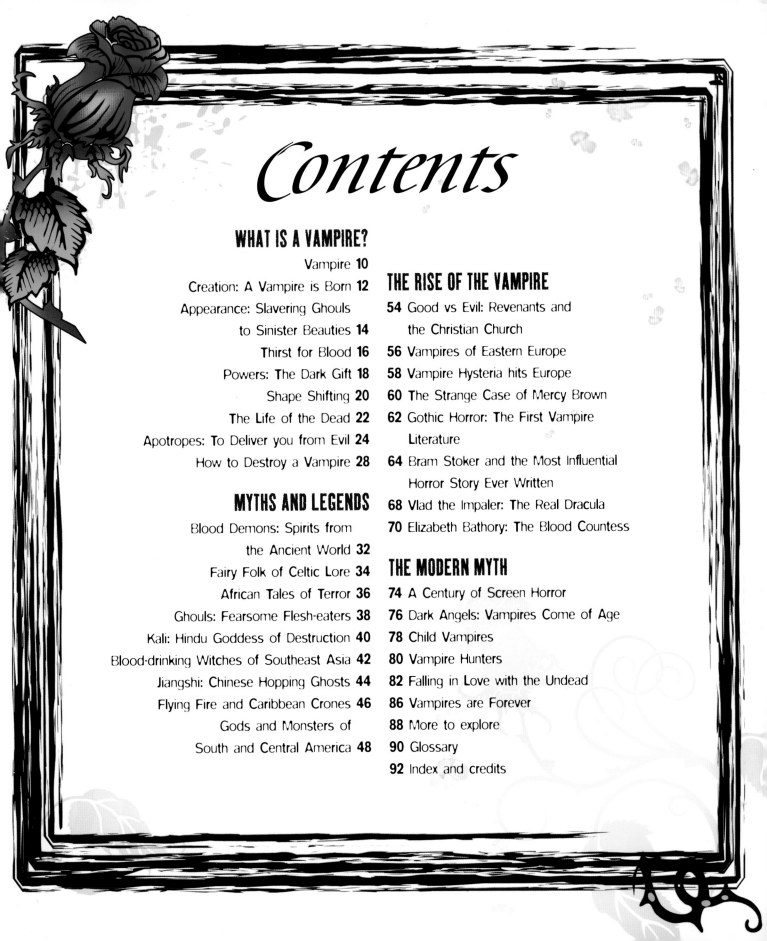

Contents

What is a Vampire?

The name vampire arouses both fear and fascination. Traditionally a dead person who leaves the grave at night to suck the blood of the living, these creatures have taken many forms over the years. They all share some basic traits, however. They thirst for blood, and have unusual powers and strengths. There are perils they must avoid, and signs that give away their deadly secret.

Vampires are forever. They are the **undead**: immortals who walk the Earth undetected, seeking blood to sustain their unnatural existence. Their origins are lost in the mists of time. From the earliest civilizations they have been whispered about in **myth** and **legend**. They have appeared in many guises. Ancient cultures all over the world feared spirits and demons that thirsted for **blood** and brought death and despair. In many places these beings were strongly associated with **witchcraft** and sorcery. Chroniclers in the Middle Ages wrote of revenants – **corpses** rising from their graves to seek blood and spread misfortune. The folklore of Eastern Europe called them **strigoi**, and belief in these restless corpses was so strong that panic would overtake any community that suspected there was one in their midst.

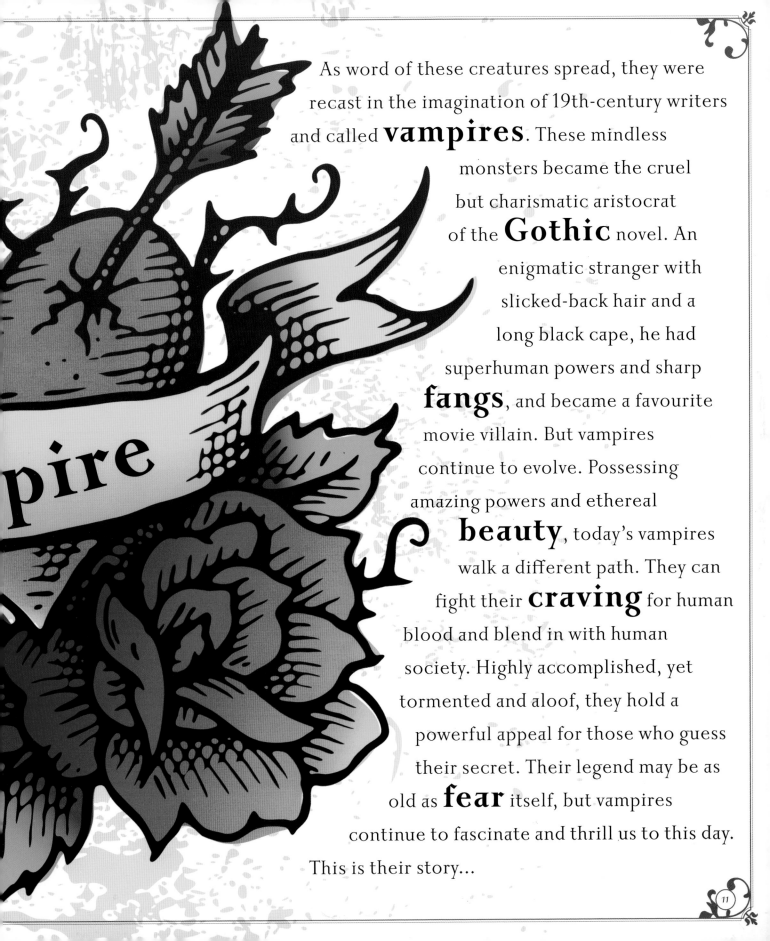

As word of these creatures spread, they were recast in the imagination of 19th-century writers and called **vampires**. These mindless monsters became the cruel but charismatic aristocrat of the **Gothic** novel. An enigmatic stranger with slicked-back hair and a long black cape, he had superhuman powers and sharp **fangs**, and became a favourite movie villain. But vampires continue to evolve. Possessing amazing powers and ethereal **beauty**, today's vampires walk a different path. They can fight their **craving** for human blood and blend in with human society. Highly accomplished, yet tormented and aloof, they hold a powerful appeal for those who guess their secret. Their legend may be as old as **fear** itself, but vampires continue to fascinate and thrill us to this day. This is their story...

Creation

— A VAMPIRE IS BORN —

There are three main ways of becoming a vampire — by birth, by death, or by bite. In folklore, the way a person entered the world, and the way they lived, died, and were buried, made the difference between eternal rest or eternal roaming. Today, it is the bite that counts.

SEALED WITH A KISS

The modern method of vampire creation is the classic act of a vampire biting into his victim to feed. As he draws blood, the bite turns the victim into one of his kind. Typically, the vampire bites into an area of the body where a main artery is near the surface — usually the neck or wrist — though in tales of folklore it could also be on the thorax or above the heart. Two small puncture marks are the only evidence of the vampire's visit, but victims will soon notice telltale signs of their fate. Their breath starts to smell, they look pale, recoil from religious artefacts, and become more active at night. Most waste away, until they die and are reborn as a new vampire. Sometimes the vampire's bite merely kills his victim, unless the victim also tastes the vampire's blood in return.

UNCERTAIN DEATH

A person's life, death, and manner of burial were crucial factors in determining vampire status in many parts of the world. Anyone committing suicide was doomed, since many religions viewed this as an unforgivable sin. Murderers, robbers, and other criminals were also seen as vulnerable to vampiric resurrection. Many cultures took the manner of laying a person to rest very seriously. If burial took place too quickly, or without the proper rituals, this was a cause for concern. In Romania, burying a person face up, or not deep enough, could result in them becoming a vampire.

DAMNED BEFORE BIRTH

A baby may seem too innocent to be labelled a vampire even before it has drawn its first breath, but in the folklore of many parts of the world, pregnancy was fraught with danger. If the mother saw a black cat, ate too much salt, or was looked at by a witch, her baby was at risk of becoming a vampire. There were also other factors to worry a mother. If the baby was born the illegitimate child of an illegitimate child, the seventh son of a seventh son, or with teeth, too much hair, or a caul (membrane) over its head, it was almost certainly destined for vampirism after death. A baby conceived or born on certain holy days would also cause its parents great anxiety.

Appearance

— SLAVERING GHOULS TO SINISTER BEAUTIES —

Vampires of old were putrid beasts — ugly, decaying corpses covered in dirt from the grave. But, refined by the imaginations of novelists and filmmakers, vampires grew ever more human, until in the 20th century they emerged as a kind of superhuman — unnaturally beautiful and fatally appealing.

A NOVEL IDEA

The fiction of the 19th century painted a different picture: suddenly vampires got class. With sunken cheeks, flowing hair, long dark fingernails, and white fangs, they were aristocratic gentlemen with skin like marble and a hungry look. The vampire was still a figure of terror, with his diabolical smile and piercing gaze, but now he was taking his place in human society and using charm to snare his victims.

DEAD UGLY

In the folklore of Eastern Europe, thought to be the origin of the modern vampire myth, blood-drinking undead beings were described as short, fat, and sweaty, with pointy ears, rat-like teeth, and rancid, stinking breath. Their bloated, rotting bodies would be dressed in rags and smeared with filth from the grave. Blood would likely trickle from their mouths. More like zombies from a horror movie, their return from death had stripped these revenants of all their recognizably human qualities.

GOLDEN OLDIE

Sporting an evening suit and a long black cape that opened out like a bat's wings, the vampire became a staple of horror movies in the 20th century. Usually an icy nobleman with a thick foreign accent, his fangs were longer, and his eyes cold and glassy, turning red with anger. Though this well-worn archetype may now seem corny, to audiences of the day these characters had huge appeal, and in the stories they often used charisma to beguile victims of the opposite sex.

TODAY'S VAMPIRE

Today's vampire could hardly be more different from the mindless ghouls of old. Modern vampires disguise their superhuman abilities to fit seamlessly into human society, and look just like us, except for being flawless in every way. There are few clues to their true nature, though their eyes change colour when they lust for blood. Those same eyes may betray their angst at an inner struggle over the life they've been blessed or cursed with.

Thirst

FOR BLOOD

Vampires are blood-drinking creatures whose very existence depends on slaking their thirst. Without a ready supply of blood they will perish. The deep, physical craving for this crimson liquid is the one characteristic that all vampires share.

ESSENCE OF LIFE

Since ancient times, people have recognized blood as the very essence of life. Egyptian princes bathed in blood to revive their mental powers, Ancient Romans drank the blood of gladiators, believing that it passed on the potency of these fierce fighters, and the Aztecs of Central America worshipped their Sun god with offerings of blood. The idea that blood was needed to sustain life made it natural to assume that "living spirits" – the undead – would also need blood, and would take it from the living.

THE THIRST

The vampire's insatiable desire for blood is known as "the thirst". All vampires need to drink fresh blood to sustain their unnatural existence. Without it, they age, weaken, and lose their powers. Starved for too long, a vampire would eventually suffer a kind of living death – conscious, but too weak to function. The vampire's need for blood is often described as being like a powerful addiction – the physical cravings for the salty, metallic substance and the feeling of strength it provides are almost impossible to resist.

FEEDING FRENZY

Historically, vampires were linked to frenzied killing sprees. Their need for blood explained to early populations why their cattle were dying, and why so many people perished in outbreaks of disease. To ingest a victim's blood, the vampire makes an incision with his razor-sharp fangs at a point on the body where a blood vessel is close to the surface. After feeding, vampires gain strength, and some even grow younger. With some restraint a vampire can return to the same victim time and again before he or she finally dies.

MODERN TASTES

Human blood gives the vampire the most strength. The blood of rats, pets, cattle, or any other animal would be enough to keep a vampire alive but would not satisfy their craving. In the modern era, some vampires have developed a conscience and a desire to live peacefully in human society. By shunning human blood and denying their craving, they battle against their very nature. By choice, these tormented souls try to make do with animal blood, but it is a poor substitute.

IMMORTALITY

Most vampires are immortal – they do not age and die as humans do. Many are also resistant to conventional weapons and the ravages of disease.

On the rare occasion a vampire is wounded, he or she heals very quickly and feels no pain.

CREATING NEW VAMPIRES

Some vampires can create more of their kind simply by feeding – their victim dies a mortal death but is reborn as one of the undead. If the creator vampire desires it, the new vampire will be enslaved, only freed if the master is weakened or destroyed.

SUPERHUMAN

A vampire possesses physical strength no human can equal. Their sheer might, coupled with the fact that they never tire, makes them extremely difficult to match in physical combat. Their power increases over time – vampires get stronger as they age.

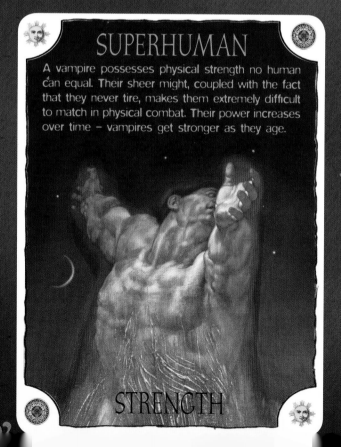

STRENGTH

Powers

— THE DARK GIFT —

Though doomed to spend eternity killing for blood, vampires are endowed with a range of extraordinary powers. Sometimes called the dark gift, each vampire's set of special abilities is different, but there are some skills all vampires share.

Control of the elements is a useful trick – a fleeing vampire can summon a storm to cover her tracks. Other magical abilities include the power to cast spells, turn base metals into gold, and shape shift into other forms.

MAGICAL ABILITIES

LIGHTNING SPEED

Vampires move with supreme grace and agility. Sometimes they move too fast for the human eye to register, seeming to appear as if from nowhere. They can defy gravity by climbing up or down the steepest walls, or leaping vertically from a standing start. Some vampires can even fly.

MIND POWERS

Using the hypnotic power of their eyes, some vampires can control the thoughts of humans and animals, compelling them to do their bidding. Some vampires can mind read, while others use telekinesis to move objects by willpower alone.

ENHANCED SENSES

Vampires are equipped with acute senses of hearing, smell, and sight. Their hearing is as sharp as a wolf's, even in the noisiest of cities. An enhanced sense of smell allows them to track their quarry, but also makes strong odours repellant. Super-sensitive eyes allow them to see clearly in total darkness.

Shape shifting

Many vampires have an extraordinary power that helps them to move about undetected. They can shape shift, or change physical form, when their human-like appearance puts them in danger. Shape shifting can involve changes of age and gender, or total transformation from human to animal form.

A bat swoops down from overhead. A wolf lurks in the shadows, eyes glinting with menace. The vampire can physically change into many shapes, but the bat and the wolf are his favourite forms.

As a bat, he can flit his way to the bedside of his victim undetected. Like the vampire, bats have a sinister appearance and only emerge at night. To our ancestors, the sight of bats flitting eerily across the sky may have echoed vampire myths. The legend was reinforced by the discovery in South America of the vampire bat, which uses razor-sharp teeth to feed on the blood of living creatures.

Appearing as a wolf, the vampire may strike even more fear into the hearts of his intended victims – he can use the animal's speed and senses to hunt them down. A fanged and dangerous predator, the wolf is the vampire's natural ally. In an urban setting, a vampire may choose to take the more familiar form of a dog.

Vampires can also morph into mice, rats, or any other animal that will help them escape destruction. Some cultures believe that when a vampire is destroyed, no bugs must be allowed to escape from the body lest the vampire survive in a different form.

And it is not only animals to watch out for. Even the green fog rolling across the lawn may be cause for disquiet. Vampires can disperse into dust, mist, or vapour to slip through door slits or keyholes.

THE
Life OF THE Dead

The vampire's way of life has changed a great deal over the centuries. No longer restricted to emerging at night from dirty coffins to terrorize cattle and villagers, the options are more varied. There is the chance to use impressive powers, mix with humans, and even enjoy their company. Some vampire traits, however, never change.

STRICT DIET

Vampires are driven by very specific dietary requirements. They require fresh blood for survival, and much of their existence is centred on getting it. Human blood is the preference of all vampires, although they can survive on the blood of lower forms of life, such as small mammals. It is said that new vampires need to feed once every two nights. Older vampires can resist their craving and survive for longer between feeds, but if any vampire goes too long without sustenance it will rapidly grow old and perish. No other food or drink ever passes their lips – they do not require it to survive and the taste of human food holds no appeal for them.

ISOLATION

Tradition says vampires make their homes in crypts, tombs, tunnels, catacombs, and old castles. They must make their resting place in their native soil, so if they wish to travel the soil must travel with them. Today, vampires suffer no such restriction and travel freely. However, those that make lives for themselves in human society are often forced to move on – either to seek new victims, or to protect their identity. This constant uprooting, and the fact that they outlive all the humans around them, can lead to a lonely and desolate existence.

CREATURES OF THE NIGHT

Vampires of legend are said to be creatures of the night. They slumber during the day, when they like to be tucked up in a grave or coffin. At dusk they stir and come to life, ready to seek out their victims. Today, vampires are more likely to lead apparently normal lives during the day, but it is in their nature to prefer hanging out at night.

A RAY OF LIGHT

It's not all doom and gloom. Many modern vampires are depicted living fulfilled, if complicated, lives. Their extraordinary powers make up for some of the downsides. They can push themselves to physical extremes, use their super-senses for a heightened appreciation of beauty, and defy gravity to see the world from different perspectives. Many have artistic talents, and can paint, sing, and play musical instruments to a high standard – they've had enough time to practise. They do not have to struggle with the mundane day-to-day concerns that occupy the human race; their lives are free of pain and illness, and they need not fear old age or death.

Apotropes

— TO DELIVER YOU FROM EVIL —

Folklore tells of many charms and tricks to ward off vampires. Apotropes are objects or substances, such as garlic, that work to repel evil. Other tactics, like the scattering of seeds, use a knowledge of the vampire's weaknesses to stop him in his tracks.

FIRE

An open flame – a burning torch or crackling campfire – might be enough to keep some vampires at bay. In many religions, fire is seen as a purifying agent. Weaker vampires hate it, as it is traditionally used to destroy them.

SILVER BULLET

Long used as a protection against evil of all kinds, silver is extremely toxic to vampires. A silver bullet is the only kind that can actually kill a vampire, but only if it goes through the heart. Silver stakes, daggers, and swords are useful in slowing a vampire's attack, while iron and lead items are also said to have a repellant effect.

GARLIC

This pungent bulb is thought to protect against disease and has been used for centuries in many parts of the world to fend off the powers of darkness. Hung around windows, or worn about the neck, garlic gives off a strong odour that will make vampires recoil.

RICE AND SEEDS

Many vampires are obsessed with counting. Grains of any kind – rice, seeds, salt, or sand – are therefore a great distraction. A vampire will be compelled to count each grain scattered on its grave or in its path.

BELLS

The incessant ringing of bells is a good way to see off a vampire – with their super-sensitive hearing the demons abhor the sound. Church bells, with their religious connotations, are particularly despised.

KNOTTED ROPE

Throwing a knotted rope or tangled net in a vampire's way has much the same effect as a scattering of seeds – the vampire will be bound to untangle each knot. Preoccupied by this, he will not be able to continue his hunt or impede your escape.

MIRRORS

Vampires are often said to have no reflection. Many believe this is due to the vampire's lack of an eternal soul. It is said that a vampire will shrink from mirrors as it hates being reminded that it is one of the undead.

WATER

Holy water is traditionally used to battle vampires – the sacred substance burns their flesh. However, it only has this effect in the hands of a true believer. Running water is also dangerous to vampires. They cannot pass over it, so are stopped immediately from giving chase.

HAWTHORN

This prickly peril could catch a vampire's cloak or shroud and stop him from moving. In Europe, dog rose, hawthorn, and blackthorn placed around the house or put in graves is said to stop a vampire in his tracks.

INVITATION

In many tales, vampires cannot enter a house unless invited. But beware, the monster does not necessarily play fair. He may disguise himself to gain entry, and, having been invited once, can then come and go as he pleases.

CHRISTIAN CROSS

Vampires hate all religious artefacts, but by far the most popular and effective repellant is the sign of the cross. Representing the death and resurrection of Jesus Christ, it is loathed by vampires. The cross is one of the few weapons that may burn a vampire's skin and cause pain.

SUNLIGHT

One of the most powerful perils, direct sunlight will weaken many vampires and cause others to crumble into dust. This sensitivity forces vampires to sleep during the day, making them extremely vulnerable if their lair is discovered.

"Whoever fights look to it that he himself a monster. And when an **abyss**, the abyss

monsters should
does not become
you gaze long into
also gazes into **you."**

Beyond Good and Evil, Friedrich Nietzsche

HOW TO *Destroy* A VAMPIRE

Vampires may seem indestructible, with their astonishing supernatural abilities. But with a cool head the well-equipped hunter can end an evil vampire's undead life for good.

FIND HIM

Vampires are fiendishly difficult to track down, but various animals can help to identify them. Dogs are likely to snarl and bark in the presence of the undead. In the folklore of Eastern Europe, a white stallion led through a graveyard was said to rear up if it reached any grave belonging to a vampire. A burial site with a blue glow or fire around it, or a plot where the earth had been disturbed, were also considered sure signs of an unnatural occupant.

CORNER HIM

Apotropaic objects should help to subdue the vamp. If a vampire's lair can be detected, holy water should be sprinkled and prayers said over it. This defiles the resting place for the vampire and prevents him from returning. Forced to live in daylight day after day, his powers would gradually diminish until eventually the vampire would crumble into dust. But beware: vampires may have more than one resting place. If you can find the beast asleep in his coffin or grave you have the ideal chance to put an end to him.

KILL HIM

A stake through the heart is the most popular way of destroying a vampire, pounded in with a mallet or the flat of a gravedigger's shovel. It's best done in one stroke, preferably using a stake made of juniper, ash, or maple wood. Vampires do not die immediately when pierced through the heart and it is possible that the monster could remove the wood during its death throes. To be sure of success, you need to decapitate the vampire and burn it to ashes. To be extra safe, the head and body must be burned separately and the ashes scattered in different locations. This prevents the monster from regenerating. Take special care not to stand in the smoke as this has the power to turn you into a vampire.

Myths and Legends

Many folk tales around the world tell of the restless dead — souls doomed to walk the earth seeking blood to sustain their existence. In the past, death wasn't necessarily seen as the end of life, but as the beginning of a new existence. This was a comfort to those left behind, but it also left a lingering doubt as to what the dead might get up to. As well as reanimated corpses, many other supernatural blood-drinkers are found in myths and legends. From ghouls and ghosts, to witches and fairies, these unearthly creatures all terrorized the living, bringing with them sickness and death.

Blood Demons

— SPIRITS FROM THE ANCIENT WORLD —

Belief in mythical blood-drinking creatures goes back at least 5,000 years to the peoples of ancient Mesopotamia. The Ancient Egyptians, Greeks, and Romans also had myths of demonic females who preyed on human life force.

LILITH

In ancient Mesopotamia, Lilith was a winged spirit of vengeance, a storm demon who brought plague and destruction and could drain men's lives with a kiss. She was later adopted into early Hebrew tradition as the first wife of Adam. In some stories she refuses to submit to Adam and flees the Garden of Eden to roam the world sucking the blood of infants.

SEKHMET

An Ancient Egyptian war goddess, Sekhmet was said to have become drunk on human blood and begun to destroy all of humanity. To stop the slaughter, the Sun god Ra gave her beer that was coloured red to imitate blood. Sekhmet then became intoxicated and was pacified. She is portrayed as a woman with a lion's head.

EKIMMU

The Ekimmu is found in the mythology of Assyria, a state established in Mesopotamia around 2,000 BCE. The spirit of a dead person unable to find peace, its name means "that which was snatched away". It is described as a person who died uncared for and was not given a proper burial.

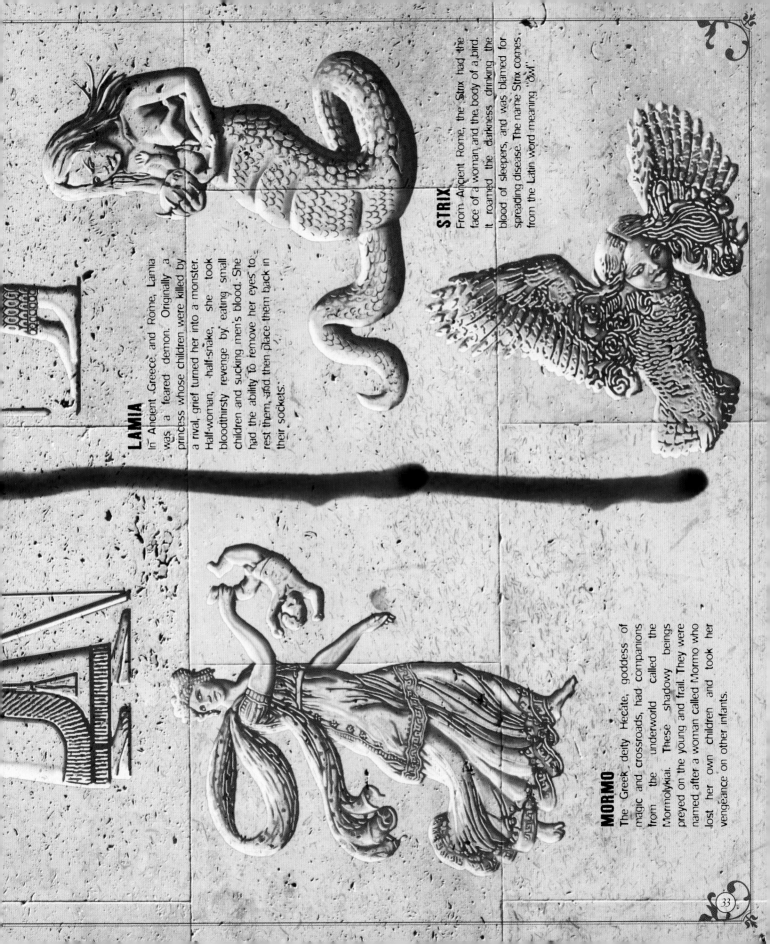

LAMIA

In Ancient Greece and Rome, Lamia was a feared demon. Originally a princess whose children were killed by a rival, grief turned her into a monster. Half-woman, half-snake, she took bloodthirsty revenge by eating small children and sucking men's blood. She had the ability to remove her eyes to rest them, and then place them back in their sockets.

STRIX

From Ancient Rome, the Strix had the face of a woman, and the body of a bird. It roamed the darkness drinking the blood of sleepers, and was blamed for spreading disease. The name Strix comes from the Latin word meaning "owl".

MORMO

The Greek deity Hecate, goddess of magic and crossroads, had companions from the underworld called the Mormolykiai. These shadowy beings preyed on the young and frail. They were named after a woman called Mormo who lost her own children and took her vengeance on other infants.

Fairy Folk

OF CELTIC LORE

The Celts were a diverse group of peoples who lived in Iron Age Europe. Traces of their religion survive in the folklore of Ireland, Scotland, and Wales, where ancient legends feature blood-sucking creatures from the fairy world. They are associated with sorcery and witchcraft, and are closely entwined with the forests and mountains where they live.

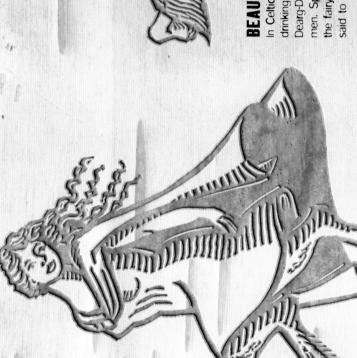

THE GREEN LADY

Half-woman and half-goat, the Glaistig or Green Lady of Scottish mythology had flowing golden hair and always wore a long green robe to hide her goat's legs. A similar fairy from the Scottish Highlands was the Baobhan Sith, which had the upper body of a beautiful woman and the hooves of a deer. Like the Banshee of Irish myth, both the Glaistig and the Baobhan Sith wailed to herald the death of important people, and were said to bewitch men into joining them in a deadly dance before feeding on their blood. They used their sharp fingernails, rather than their teeth, to draw the blood of their victims.

BEAUTIFUL BUT DEADLY

In Celtic folklore there are many beautiful, blood-drinking fairy women. The Leanan Sidhe and Dearg-Due of Irish myth would enslave mortal men. Spellbound, the men would waste away as the fairy lived off their blood. Often the victim was said to go mad before their premature death.

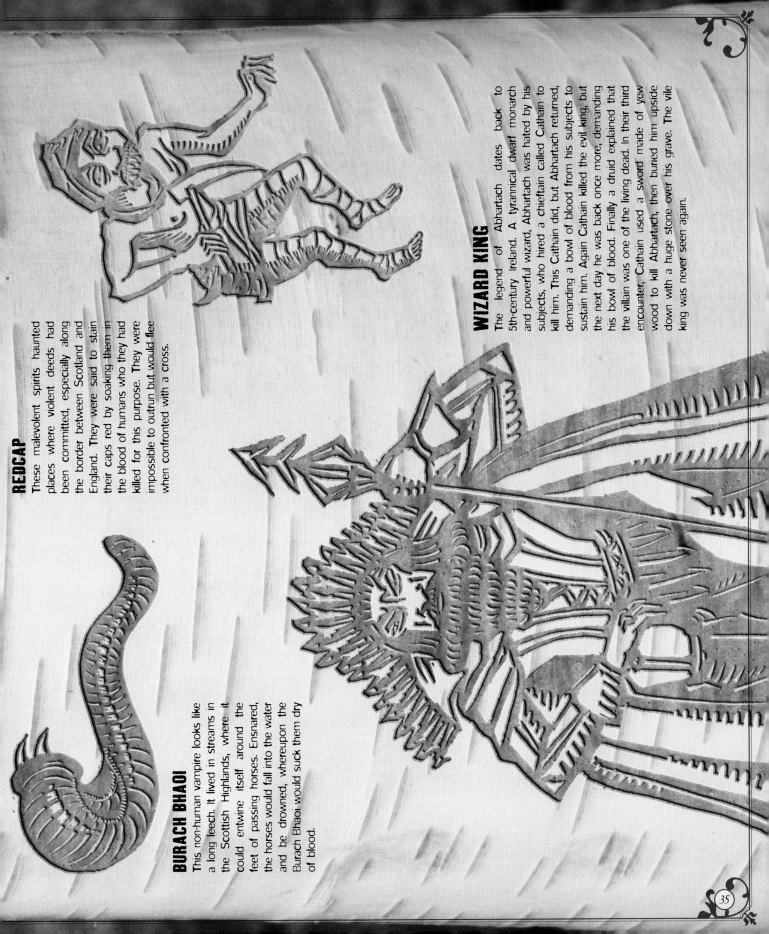

REDCAP

These malevolent spirits haunted places where violent deeds had been committed, especially along the border between Scotland and England. They were said to stain their caps red by soaking them in the blood of humans who they had killed for this purpose. They were impossible to outrun but would flee when confronted with a cross.

BURACH BHAOI

This non-human vampire looks like a long leech. It lived in streams in the Scottish Highlands, where it could entwine itself around the feet of passing horses. Ensnared, the horses would fall into the water and be drowned, whereupon the Burach Bhaoi would suck them dry of blood.

WIZARD KING

The legend of Abhartach dates back to 5th-century Ireland. A tyrannical dwarf monarch and powerful wizard, Abhartach was hated by his subjects, who hired a chieftain called Cathain to kill him. This Cathain did, but Abhartach returned, demanding a bowl of blood from his subjects to sustain him. Again Cathain killed the evil king, but the next day he was back once more, demanding his bowl of blood. Finally a druid explained that the villain was one of the living dead. In their third encounter, Cathain used a sword made of yew wood to kill Abhartach, then buried him upside down with a huge stone over his grave. The vile king was never seen again.

African

On the African continent, blood-drinking and flesh-eating creatures come in many different guises. Most are not undead, but living souls who dwell unrecognized in their unfortunate communities.

ADZE

In southeastern Ghana, people of the Ewe tribe believed sorcerers living among them to be host to a vampire spirit known as the Adze. Resembling a firefly, it would drink coconut water and palm oil, but most of all it sought the blood of young children. If caught, it would quickly revert to human form.

OBAYIFO

A witch-like person who lived secretly among the Ashanti people of Ghana, the Obayifo becomes a glowing ball during the hours of darkness, when she seeks the blood of children. A bad harvest would also be blamed on the Obayifo – she is obsessed with food, and partial to sucking the juice out of fruit and vegetables.

ASANBOSAM

This creature was said to live deep in the forests of southern Ghana. It looked almost human, but had hooks on its legs and ferocious iron teeth. Dangling from trees it would snatch up passers-by, who were usually hunters, to feast on their blood. In some regions the Asanbosam attacked sleeping villagers by biting them on the thumb.

IMPUNDULU

The Zulu and Xhosa tribes of South Africa believed in a creature called the Impundulu, or "lightning bird". This giant black-and-white beast is said to summon thunder and lightning with its wings and talons. It was usually the servant of a witch, who would use its unquenchable thirst for blood to destroy her enemies.

ZOMBIES

These terrifying creatures are incredibly strong, and rip their victims apart before consuming their flesh. They are found in Voodoo – a religion that developed on the Caribbean island of Haiti based on the spiritual beliefs of West African peoples. In Voodoo tradition, zombies are corpses that have been reanimated by priests to become mindless servants, doomed to toil forever under the will of their master.

SOUL-EATERS

Folklore of the Hausa tribe of West Africa tells of witches called soul-eaters, who preyed on their victims' life force. The soul-eater could shape shift into animals so peculiar-looking that they would startle any onlooker to the point where their soul would leap out of their body and be gobbled up. The soulless victim would then waste away.

Ghouls

— FEARSOME FLESH-EATERS —

Out of the Arabian Desert came monsters called ghouls. These diabolical spirits had an insatiable appetite for blood and flesh. Nocturnal, with regenerative powers that made them difficult to kill, they shared many traits with vampires. A person was thought to become a ghoul after death as a result of living a wicked life.

DESERT DEMON

Ghouls were said to be the offspring of Iblis, the Islamic equivalent of Satan – their name comes from an Arabic word meaning "demon". In folk tales from the Arabian Peninsula, ghouls ranged from mindless beasts to those that passed as human during the day, living seemingly normal lives but coming out at night to hunt. All were said to have the ability to shape shift into any form, particularly favouring scavengers such as the hyena. Strong and fast, they experienced no pain, did not age, and did not require air to breathe. The only way to kill them was with a sharp blow to the head.

WEARY TRAVELLERS

Travellers planning to cross the vast expanse of the Arabian Desert needed to be wary of ghouls. These evil spirits could materialize out of nowhere and command the minds of their victims, luring weary men away from the safety of their group. They would then attack ferociously with tooth and claw. Greatly feared, ghouls were often associated with the spread of disease – some believed that even the touch of a ghoul could be deadly.

GRAVEYARD SHIFT

Traditionally, ghouls were said to live underground or in creeks and ditches. They prefered to eat fresh meat, especially that of children, but if this was in short supply they would gather in cemeteries to feast on corpses.

Kali

— HINDU GODDESS OF DESTRUCTION —

The Hindu deity Kali is the goddess of destruction and pestilence, and is famed for her taste for blood. She inspires fear but is also honoured as representing time and change. She is just one of many blood-drinkers in Indian mythology.

GODDESS OF DESTRUCTION

Often depicted as a woman with four arms, fangs, and a long tongue, Kali is a terrifying figure. With one hand she clutches a sword, while with another she holds the head of a slain giant. Around her neck she wears a necklace of skulls. She is often depicted standing on Shiva, her companion deity. The story goes that Kali was fighting the demon Raktavija, but every drop of his blood that spilled on the battlefield turned into a new demon, until the battlefield was filled with thousands of them. To defeat Raktavija, Kali sucked the blood straight from his body and devoured the demons. Drunk on her success, Kali got carried away and started destroying everything in sight, so Shiva threw himself beneath her feet in order to stop the destruction.

MYTH TO RELIGION

Kali is just one of many bloodthirsty creatures in Indian mythology, originating in the magic and superstition of ancient traditions. Hinduism – which developed in the Indus Valley (in modern-day Pakistan) and spread across India around 1000 BCE – was tolerant and accepting of these long-held folk beliefs and enabled them to spread thoughout the land. Some creatures, like Kali, were incorporated into the religion and became ferocious gods. Others live on in folk traditions.

GRAVEYARD GHOULS

Indian tradition tells of many flesh-eating ghouls that lurk in burial grounds. In Hindu mythology Vetalas (also known as Baital) are spirits that live in recently deceased corpses. At night they search for the blood of sleeping, drunk, or mad women. They look like old women, deformed by discoloured skin and poisoned fingernails. Bhutas are wandering souls that also live in graveyards. They are thought to be the spirits of dead people who did not receive proper funeral rites. They can shape shift into bats and attack the living to cause disease. Rakshasas are man-eating spirits, first described in the Atharva Veda (a Hindu religious text). They appear in many guises, usually as a half-human, half-animal creature covered in blood.

FEMALE FRIGHTS

Females who seek vengeance from beyond the grave proliferate in Indian mythology. The Churel was believed to be a woman who had died in pregnancy during the important Divali festival. She returns to suck the blood of her relatives. The Churel is a gruesome sight, with feet pointing backwards and a protruding black tongue. Another fearsome female was the Masani. Inhabiting burial grounds, this spirit was black in appearance due to the ash from her funeral pyre. She hunted at night, attacking anyone who passed by. Though there are many ghoulish spirits in Indian mythology, some are not entirely evil. The Pisacha, for example, are demons that eat corpses, but can also restore the sick to health if enticed.

BLOOD-DRINKING
Witches
OF SOUTHEAST ASIA

Across Southeast Asia, blood-drinking creatures are strongly associated with black magic. Dark tales abound of beautiful but bloodthirsty witches and sorcerer's slaves.

MONSTROUS MAIDEN

The Penanggalan is one of the most gruesome of all mythical creatures. This terrible ghoul looks like a beautiful maiden during the day, but at night her head detaches from her body and flies around, intestines dangling beneath, seeking the blood of newborn infants. At the end of the night, the Penanggalan must use a vat of vinegar to shrink her swollen innards so they will fit back into her body.

GHASTLY GOBLIN

While many Asian vampires feed on infants, the Toyol actually is a baby, albeit an enchanted one. Brought to life by a sorcerer, the creature resembles a small goblin. It is strong and mischievous, and must be kept in a jar all day with an offering of fresh blood each night. In return, it will do its master's bidding – especially stealing. If a Toyol escapes, it sucks the toes of sleepers leaving small bite marks.

FLYING FIENDS

A beautiful older woman with huge, bat-like wings, the Manananggal can separate the top half of her body from the bottom half. If her lower half is found while she is out on a night's hunt for blood, it can be smothered in garlic or salt, preventing the Manananggal from rejoining it. The Aswang, a related vampire from the Philippines, is also an attractive female who flies through the night. Landing on a roof, she uses her long, pointed tongue to pierce the skin of the sleeping victim below.

NOT ALL THERE

The Pontianak is described as tall and graceful, with long, black hair cascading to her ankles. She is so beautiful that her victims fall under her spell, but her long hair hides a secret – a huge hole in her back. The Pontianak can turn into a screech owl at night and paralyze victims with its awful sound, before feeding on them. It is sensitive to sunlight, and will die if exposed for too long. A similar vampire is the Langsuir, who also has a gaping hole in her back. Both these witches prefer the blood of babies.

Jiangshi

— CHINESE HOPPING GHOSTS —

Covered in hair, with razor-sharp talons and dagger-like teeth, these lost souls are often called Chinese vampires. Named jiangshi, or "hopping ghosts", they would attack at night, leaping from their graves to suck the life force from their hapless victims.

SPLIT SOUL

According to Chinese belief, each person has two souls: the higher soul, or hun, and the lower soul, or p'o. After death, the hun ascends to join the spirit world. But if a person lived a bad life, their p'o would remain earthbound, trapped in the body, which would be reanimated as a jiangshi. Liars, cheats, and those who committed suicide were particularly vulnerable. What happened after death was also significant, however. A blameless person who was not given a proper funeral could become a jiangshi, and an animal leaping over the corpse could also condemn the unfortunate soul to join the ranks of the undead. The utmost care had to be taken when preparing the body for burial lest the deceased's spirit was sullied: even leaning over a body was considered risky.

BOUND TO HOP

The name "hopping ghost" stems from the Chinese tradition of burying the dead in special garments that tied the legs together. The creature, having risen from the dead in its funeral garb, would then have to hop to move around. Another explanation is that the dead were often transported from the towns where they worked back to the place of their birth. Carried upright on bamboo stretchers, the corpses appeared to be bobbing up and down.

FEROCIOUS FIEND

The jiangshi's appearance ranged from human-like to gruesome with a long black tongue and eyeballs hanging out of their sockets. Jiangshi were said to be blind, foul-smelling, and entirely covered with long green or white hair. Their incredibly long eyebrows could be used to lasso their victims, who would then be ripped limb from limb and devoured.

VANQUISHING A VAMPIRE

Many folk tales and legends featured the jiangshi – usually, unsuspecting travellers would disturb the creature's rest and meet a horrible fate. There were ways to keep the creature at bay though. Loud noises, such as thunder, could kill them. Straw and chicken blood would repel them, garlic burned their skin, and piles of sticky rice would snare them. They liked to count, so red peas were a useful distraction. Many stories featured a mythical figure called Zhong Kui, who battled the fearsome jiangshi. Cheated out of first place in his civil service exams, he was said to have committed suicide in front of the Imperial Palace. The emperor honoured him with an imperial burial, and out of gratitude Zhong Kui's spirit promised to rid the world of ghosts and demons with his magic sword. His fierce image is often painted on Chinese houses as a talisman of good luck.

Flying Fire

AND CARIBBEAN CRONES

The islands of the Caribbean have many myths of creatures that feed on blood, but most common is the legend of the vampire witch. During the day, she lives unnoticed in the community but at night she transforms to wreak terror on her neighbours.

SKINLESS HAG

In Jamaica, she is known as Ol'higue, or "old suck". During the day, Ol'higue looks like a frail old woman, but at night this seemingly harmless spinster sheds her skin and turns into a flying ball of fire on the lookout for blood, particularly that of newborn babies. Once she has located her prey, the hideous creature shifts back into an old woman, but without her skin, and sucks the baby's blood. If anyone in the community suspected a woman was such a creature, the children would cry "ole higue" at her, and make chalk marks on her door. A trap would be set beside the cot of potential victims – a simple heap of rice grains and the scent of a spice called asafoetida. Together these items could cast a spell on the witch, compelling her to count each grain of rice. If dawn broke before she could return to her skin, the enraged locals would pounce on her and beat her to death.

PACT WITH THE DEVIL

Grenada's version of the monster is called the Lagaroo or Loogaroo. The Lagaroo is in league with the Devil. She can perform magic, but only if she pays the Devil in blood every night. She is forced to seek the blood of others, because if she gave her own she would die. She looks like a sweet old granny in daylight hours, but at night she sheds her skin – usually leaving it under a "Devil Tree", a silk cotton tree – to become a flying ball of flame that haunts the night. After she has collected enough blood she can return to her skin and change back into human form. If her skin is taken away from the Devil Tree so that she cannot find it, she will perish.

SALT HER SKIN

Trinidad's vampire witch is called a Soucouyant. This old woman also sheds her skin at night and travels as a bright ball of light, searching out sleeping victims. Two little bite marks left side by side on the skin are a telltale sign of a nocturnal visit by a Soucouyant. If you know the identity of the crone, the solution is simple. After she leaves her house at night, her skin must be taken and rubbed with salt and pepper. The agony this causes leads her to cease her evil doings. Otherwise, the only recourse is to beat the flying flame violently with sticks. The next morning a woman looking battered and bruised would be revealed as the Soucouyant.

GODS AND *Monsters*
OF SOUTH AND CENTRAL AMERICA

For the ancient peoples of South and Central America, blood-drinking creatures held great power. For some, these strange beings were the remnants of evil spirits who were hostile to mankind. For others they were important deities, to be feared and worshipped.

CIHUATETEO
The Aztecs of Mexico believed in a vampire spirit called Cihuateteo. A woman who had died in childbirth, she returned after death to plague the living, especially infants. People would leave her offerings of blood in the hope that she would spare their children.

ASEMA
The Asema of Surinam was a kind of "living vampire", an old man or woman who could take off its skin and become a ball of light at night. After it found its sleeping victim, it would revert to human form to feed on his or her blood.

LOBISHOMEN

Tiny in stature, the Lobishomen of Brazilian folklore resembled a bald-headed monkey. A kind of blood-sucking werewolf, it was hunch-backed with bloodless lips, yellow skin, and black teeth. Padded feet helped it creep up quietly on the women it would attack.

PISHTACO

Native to Peru, the Pishtaco does not immediately feed off blood. First it gorges on fat, and only when sated does it move on to drink blood. This creature operated at night and could take on the form of a vampire bat.

JARACACA

The Jaracaca of Brazilian mythology does drink blood, but it prefers human milk. Taking on the form of a snake, it slides through the jungle unobserved and stalks nursing mothers. Its spit and venom cause insanity, so it is greatly feared.

CAMAZOTZ

The Maya of Central America worshipped a deity called Camazotz. He had the body of a man and the head and wings of a bat, and presided over the cycle of crops. Powerful and malignant, he was thirsty for blood, and lurked in caves.

"...it is hard to believe that had **so complete a** old and young, in all parts of history, has not some **terrible truth...**"

a phenomenon which has **hold** over nations both of the world, at all times underlying and

The Vampire: His Kith and Kin, Montague Summers

Rise of the ◆ Vampire

The vampire we are familiar with first took shape in the folklore of Eastern Europe. Isolated village communities blamed the spread of disease and crop failure on the undead, who they believed rose from their graves to suck the blood of the living. Stories of hysterical villagers digging up and staking bodies began to spread west, sparking the imagination of writers and poets. In the fiction of the 19th century, the slavering ghoul of myth was transformed into the cruel count – a monster with a more human face, but an intent just as evil.

Good vs Evil

— REVENANTS AND THE CHRISTIAN CHURCH —

In Medieval Europe, death and disease were often attributed to revenants – the dead who rise from their graves. As the Christian Church gained in strength, it explained these undead creatures as the work of the Devil. By incorporating them into Christian teachings about sin and the afterlife, the Church strengthened beliefs in the restless dead and emphasized the triumph of good over evil.

PAGAN BELIEFS

Folk belief in the vengeful dead had existed in Europe long before the Christian Church came to prominence, often linked to witchcraft and sorcery. In the Middle Ages many peasants still held to these pagan ideas. The Church wanted to end paganism and witchcraft, and began to absorb elements of these beliefs, explaining them instead as the work of Satan.

RAMPAGING REVENANTS

Medieval Europe was plagued by famine and disease. The Black Death swept across the continent in waves between 1300 and 1700, laying waste to whole villages. When these bouts of mass sickness struck, or when crops failed or livestock perished, some blamed the restless soul of a recently deceased member of the community. These revenants were believed to spread disease and misfortune.

POWER OF THE CROSS

The Church believed it alone had the power to rid communities of revenants. Priests were uniquely placed to fight these minions of the Devil. The crucifix, symbolizing the Christian faith and the resurrection of Jesus Christ, and holy water, blessed by a priest, were all that were needed to force out evil.

SACRED RITES

The Christian faith involves blood rituals of its own. When Christians celebrate the Eucharist, or Holy Communion, they eat bread and drink wine that represent the body and blood of Jesus Christ. This commemorates the Last Supper and is thought to bestow God's grace upon believers.

WILLIAM OF NEWBURGH

Stories of revenants were committed to print by many Christian chroniclers. One of these was William of Newburgh, a 12th-century English churchman and historian. In his *History of English Affairs* he included accounts of people returning from the dead to plague their neighbours.

Vampires
OF EASTERN EUROPE

In the 16th and 17th centuries, the countries of Eastern Europe were rife with myths of blood-drinking revenants. These horrific reanimated corpses later came to be known as vampires. In Romania and Slovakia, belief in them was so strong that graves were desecrated and bodies staked in an effort to root them out.

THE RESTLESS DEAD

In the rural communities of Romania and Slovakia, people held strong beliefs about the walking dead. When misfortune, disease, or food shortages struck, these were often attributed to the deceased who, unable to rest in their graves, had risen up to inflict evil on their neighbours. Known variously as strigoi and moroi, these creatures were said to prowl at night and feed on blood. Little more than reanimated corpses, they were bloated and swollen with ruddy skin and staring eyes. Once human, in death these people had become hideous-looking monsters. When someone was suspected of being a vampire, locals would dig up the body. If the corpse seemed suspiciously fresh-looking, or there were trickles of blood at the mouth and nose, this was taken as confirmation. Frightened villagers would thrust a stake through the body, or remove the heart and burn it.

PREVENTION BETTER THAN CURE

In Romania, a relative of the deceased would carry wine and bread to the grave to appease the corpse and prevent vampiric activity. Slovakians would send elderly women to the cemetery to stick five hawthorn pegs or old knives into the grave, one at the position of the deceased's chest, and the other four at each limb – to pin down a vampire attempting to rise from the grave. Weighing the eyes down with coins, tying the mouth closed, or stuffing the mouth with garlic were also common practices. If this failed, the peasants would send for a dhampir. Said to be half-vampire, half-human, dhampirs were uniquely capable of combatting vampires, and would use stakes, decapitation, garlic, holy symbols, and fire to destroy the monster.

FATE WORSE THAN DEATH

There were many theories as to why a person would become a vampire. In Romania the seventh son born to a seventh son was thought to be doomed to an afterlife as one of the undead. Babies born with teeth or a caul (membrane) over their heads were similarly fated. Others who were thought to be susceptible were those with red hair and blue eyes, criminals, suicides, and those who did not receive a proper funeral.

VAMPIRE
Hysteria
HITS EUROPE

Vampire legends were everywhere in Eastern Europe, but the outside world only began to take an interest when the stories were officially investigated and reported in newspapers. The gruesome tales soon spread, and Europe went vampire mad.

EXPERT OPINION

In 1718, a peace treaty called the Peace of Passarowitz was agreed between the warring Ottoman and Habsburg empires. Under the treaty, parts of Serbia and Wallachia were turned over to the Austrian Habsburgs. The new occupying forces began to notice, investigate, and report on the peculiar local practices of exhuming bodies and "killing" them. When these happenings were reported in books and newspapers, people in Western Europe became aware for the first time of rituals that had been going on for hundreds of years.

POOR PETER

One of the first to be mentioned in an official report was Peter Plogojowitz from Serbia. After his death in 1725 nine people fell ill and died, claiming on their deathbeds that Plogojowitz had come to them in their sleep and tried to strangle them. When Plogojowitz was dug up, Austrian officials witnessed the proceedings. They found his body had not decomposed, and there was fresh blood at his mouth – signs they took as evidence of vampirism. The corpse was staked and burned, and Peter became famous across Europe.

ARNOLD PAOLE

Another well-documented case was that of Arnold Paole from Belgrade, Serbia. In 1727 Paole died soon after telling his fiancée he had encountered an undead being. When four villagers died in quick succession, Paole was blamed. Villagers exhumed his body and drove a stake through his heart. The Austrian authorities sent army doctor Johann Flückinger to investigate. He wrote a famous report of the vampire incidents known as *Visum et Repertum* ("Seen and Discovered"), which was read with keen interest all over Western Europe.

VAMPIRE MANIA

The reports on Paole and Plogojowitz caused a sensation. Books were written about the subject, the most famous by French monk Dom Augustin Calmet. But not everyone believed in the claims – French thinker Voltaire dismissed them as nonsense. The controversy only ceased when Empress Maria Theresa of Austria sent her personal physician to investigate. He concluded that vampires did not exist, and the Empress passed laws banning the opening of graves and desecration of bodies. Things calmed down, but the legend refused to die.

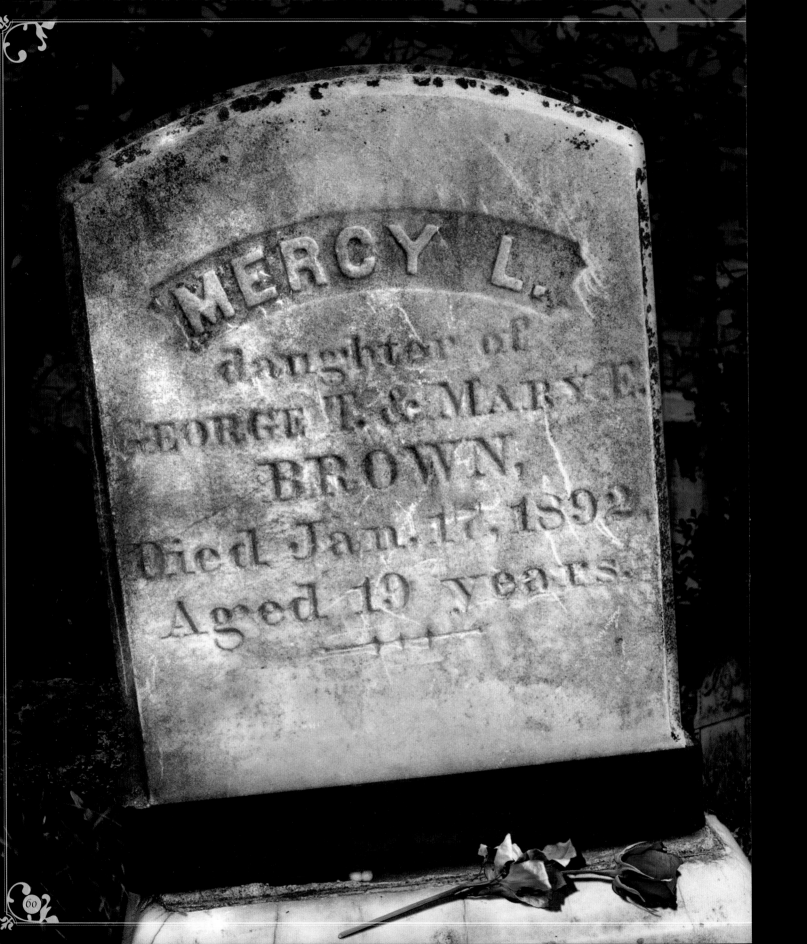

The Strange Case of Mercy Brown

RHODE ISLAND, MARCH 1892

Mercy Lena Brown was born in 1873 in Rhode Island, the daughter of farmer George T Brown and his wife Mary. She had one brother and four sisters, and the family lived outside of the small town of Exeter. When Mercy was just 10 years old her mother Mary died following a short illness. Two years later, her oldest sister, Mary Olive, began complaining of terrifying dreams and a crushing weight on her chest. She too soon perished.

Another five years passed and Mercy's brother Edwin became the next family member to fall ill. He complained of suffocation at night and became a pale wreck. Sent away to recover, his health immediately improved. But when he returned home he found the family in mourning once again: Mercy had died.

She was laid to rest in Chestnut Hill Cemetery. But she was not fated to rest in peace. Locals started whispering: they said they felt weak and had dreamed of Mercy. Edwin began to get sick again. He felt the weight on his chest and started coughing up blood.

Old European folk tales, brought to America by those who had emigrated there, and passed down from generation to generation, told of the restless dead – people whose spirits would rise up to torment the living. They would feed off surviving family members, sapping their life force until eventually the victims wasted away altogether. Similar outbreaks in the state had also been ascribed to the work of vampires. To the townspeople, the solution seemed clear: Mercy had to be exhumed.

Reluctantly, George Brown agreed that the bodies of his family should be dug up, to identify which one was causing the affliction. On 19th March 1892, a crowd gathered in the churchyard to witness the gruesome task, which was led by a local doctor. All that remained of Mercy's mother and sister were dry bones, but Mercy, who had died only two months earlier, looked shockingly lifelike. Her heart was removed and found to be full of blood.

This was all the proof the townspeople needed that Mercy was indeed a vampire. Her heart was burned at a nearby rock and the ashes were mixed with water and given to Edwin to drink. It was to no avail – he died just a few days later – but his was the last suspicious death. The family curse had been lifted.

Stop Press!

A local newspaper, *The Providence Journal*, printed a lurid account of the gathering at Mercy's grave. The story was picked up by the press in other parts of the US, and though many of the reports were mocking of the Rhode Islanders' superstitions, the coverage helped Mercy's tale go down in local lore. Today her legend lives on, with her grave attracting ghost-hunters and fright-fans to this day.

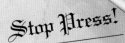

Deadly Disease

In the years after Mercy's death, a more mundane explanation of events came to light. The deaths in the Brown family were caused by tuberculosis – a disease both deadly and highly contagious. Sufferers coughed blood, felt a weight on the chest, and became pale, thin, and tired – as if they were simply wasting away. Mercy died in the middle of a New England winter, when the ground was frozen and a grave couldn't be dug. Her body was kept in an outhouse on the outskirts of the cemetery (pictured above). In the icy conditions, it is not surprising that her body was well preserved two months later.

THE
VAMPYRE;
A TALE

JOHN POLIDORI
(1819)

THE BRIDE
OF THE
ISLES

J R PLANCHÉ
(1820)

VARNEY
THE VAMPIRE
OR, THE FEAST OF BLOOD

JAMES MALCOLM RYMER
(1840)

CARMILLA

SHERIDAN LE FANU
(1872)

GOOD
LADY
DUCAYNE

M E BRADDON
(1896)

Gothic Horror

— THE FIRST VAMPIRE LITERATURE —

The vampire stories that emerged from Eastern Europe in the 18th century thrilled the chattering classes of Paris and London. But it wasn't until the early 19th century that vampires first appeared in fiction, satisfying the public's appetite for Gothic horror. No longer bloated corpses, these vampires were aristocratic, pale, and romantic.

A VAMPYRIC TALE

The first vampire novel was dreamed up in 1816 during a ghost-writing session near Lake Geneva, Switzerland, between writer Mary Shelley and Romantic poet Lord Byron. Shelley came up with *Frankenstein*, which became another classic of the horror genre, while Byron began a tale of an aristocrat who dies in Turkey and promises to return from the dead. Byron never finished the work, but his physician, Dr John Polidori, did. Published in 1819, *The Vampyre* featured Lord Ruthven, a nobleman with a thirst for blood and more than a trace of Byron's own dashing but dangerous persona.

RUTHVEN TREADS THE BOARDS

Polidori's tale was adapted for the stage in 1820 by J R Planché as *The Vampire, or The Bride of the Isles*. Among the many embellishments of the story, the setting was transferred to Scotland and Lord Ruthven appeared on stage in a kilt and tam-o'-shanter. A specially built trapdoor, still known in the theatre as a "vampire trap", allowed the vampire to rise up from his tomb through the stage floor, terrifying an audience unused to such technical tricks.

THE NEVER-ENDING STORY

The next landmark vampire story was a serialized publication that ran to 868 pages, divided into 220 chapters. Issued in lurid colours, it told of the distinctly repetitive adventures of Sir Francis Varney. In each chapter, Varney tries to seduce an innocent girl, before the locals realize he is a vampire and go after him. Eventually Varney commits suicide by jumping into a volcano. The first literary vampire to have fangs, Varney was also the first to shape shift into a wolf, have hypnotic powers and superhuman strength, and be virtually indestructible.

FEMME FATALE

In 1872 Irish writer Sheridan Le Fanu offered a new take on the genre by making his lead character female. Carmilla appears to be young but is actually a 200-year-old aristocrat. She befriends a young girl named Laura, who slowly wastes away. Family and friends finally put two and two together, and after locating Carmilla's tomb, they strike her head from her body and stake her through the heart. Possessed of amazing strength, Carmilla can shape shift, stalking her prey in the form of a black cat. In a twist that soon became familiar in vampire fiction, Le Fanu's lead character was at once horrifying and intensely desirable.

GOOD LADY, BAD BLOODLETTING

Mary Elizabeth Braddon's short story *Good Lady Ducayne*, published in 1896, brought the vampire tale bang up to date. Young Bella Rolleston, who needs a job but has no qualifications, is hired as a companion to the amiable Lady Ducayne. Her employer's previous companions have mysteriously wasted away and died, whilst the ancient lady seems to thrive. On a visit to Italy, Bella, too, begins to weaken. Fortunately her friend Stafford realizes that Lady Ducayne has been siphoning off the young girls' blood to keep her alive, using the new medical process of transfusion to transfer their blood into her own veins in an attempt to become young and beautiful again.

BRAM STOKER

AND THE MOST
INFLUENTIAL HORROR STORY EVER WRITTEN

Bram Stoker was born in Ireland in 1847. He was a sickly child, and his imagination was fired by the gruesome folk tales his mother would tell at his bedside to amuse him. As an adult he moved to London and became business manager of the famous Lyceum Theatre. To the outside world he was a jovial man, but inside he was preoccupied with disturbing thoughts. It is said that a nightmare of being attacked by three vampiric women gave him the idea for a novel...

Bram as a boy

Stoker had already written a few horror stories, but this was to be very different. He spent years reading everything he could on vampires – from folk myths to novels such as *The Vampyre* and *Carmilla*. He travelled to the seaside town of Whitby, where he talked to local fishermen about shipwrecks. In Whitby's library he found a book on the old Romanian state of Wallachia, which mentioned the Carpathian Mountains and the bloody history of Vlad the Impaler. All the while he was surrounded by theatricality, working at the Lyceum with the famous Victorian actor, Sir Henry Irving, whose physical characteristics and mannerisms inspired Stoker's central character.

Dracula was finally published in June 1897. Told through a series of letters and diary entries, the story revolved around Count Dracula, a smartly dressed aristocrat who lives in a gloomy castle. He is a creature from the past, more than 400 years old, who claims to be a descendent of Attila the Hun. Drawing on Eastern European myths, Stoker made his blood-drinking villain repelled by garlic and religious artefacts, able to shape shift, only capable of entering a house when invited, and vulnerable to a stake through the heart. From his own imagination, Stoker endowed his creation with enormous strength and the ability to crawl up walls.

When the book was first released, it received a mixed response. Some reviewers found it distasteful, and Stoker made little money from it in his lifetime. But with its transition to the stage, and subsequently film, the book became a huge success. By the 1940s it had sold more than a million copies, and since then it has never been out of print. By making the myth more believable to a modern audience, Bram Stoker catapulted the vampire to a whole new level of fame.

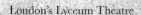

London's Lyceum Theatre

DRACULA: THE STORY IN BRIEF

Bram Stoker's novel opens with the journey of young solicitor Jonathan Harker, who has been sent to visit the mysterious Count Dracula at his castle in remote Transylvania. While helping him to finalize the purchase of a house in England, Jonathan is at first charmed by the Count. However, he soon finds he is imprisoned in the creepy castle and that his host is, in fact, a vampire.

With the young solicitor incarcerated, Dracula sets off for England on board a ship called the *Demeter*. On the journey, all the crew perish in unexplained circumstances and the ship runs aground on the English coast at Whitby, Yorkshire, where Jonathan's fiancée Mina Murray and her friend Lucy Westenra happen to be staying. Lucy falls prey to the vampire and, on her return to London, begins to waste away. Her fiancé, Arthur Holmwood, and two former suitors,

Dr Seward and Quincey Morris, are determined to save her, and call on the assistance of Professor Van Helsing. When Lucy dies, Van Helsing realizes she has become a vampire and helps the men put an end to her.

The evil Count

In Dr Seward's asylum, located near Carfax Abbey, Dracula's new home, the inmate Renfield begins to act in increasingly strange ways. Van Helsing, Mina, Jonathan (who has escaped from Transylvania), Arthur, Quincey, and Seward come together to hunt for the vampire. But the malevolent Count has made Mina his next victim. The men pursue Dracula back to Transylvania, where in a final battle they stab him through the heart and decapitate him – killing him once and for all, and freeing Mina from his clutches.

LIST OF KEY CHARACTERS

COUNT DRACULA: A nobleman and powerful vampire.

JONATHAN HARKER: A young solicitor from London, he is sent to Transylvania to advise Dracula on a property deal.

MINA MURRAY: Jonathan's fiancée, later his wife.

LUCY WESTENRA: Mina's best friend. She falls under Dracula's spell and becomes one of the undead.

PROFESSOR ABRAHAM VAN HELSING: A Dutch scientist and vampire expert, he leads the fight against Dracula.

DR JOHN SEWARD: The doctor who runs the asylum that becomes the headquarters for the vampire-fighting team.

ARTHUR HOLMWOOD: Becomes Lucy's fiancé and finances the vampire hunt.

QUINCEY P MORRIS: A rich young American. He is in love with Lucy, and is committed to the fight against Dracula.

R M RENFIELD: An inmate in Dr Seward's insane asylum. He hails Dracula as his "Master".

Carfax Abbey, where Dracula sets up home

"I could feel the hot breath on my neck. Then the skin of my throat began to tingle...

I could feel the soft, shivering touch of the lips on the super sensitive skin of my throat, and the hard dents of two sharp teeth."

Dracula, Bram Stoker

VLAD THE *Impaler*
— THE REAL DRACULA —

Ruler of the mountainous principality of Wallachia, a region of modern-day Romania, Vlad Dracula was a bloody tyrant who struck fear into the hearts of his own people. Bram Stoker used his name for his famous fictional villain, though many believe the novel owes Vlad's violent legend much more besides.

VLAD THE BAD

Born in 1431, Vlad Dracula had a turbulent upbringing, spending much of his boyhood as a hostage of the Ottoman Empire. He came to the throne in 1448, but his reign was interrupted twice before his death in 1476. He is regarded as one of the nastiest rulers in history, coming to be known as Vlad Tepes (pronounced tse-pesh), which means "the impaler".

WALLACHIA

The Medieval principality of Wallachia was a small territory sandwiched uneasily between two powerful warring empires: the Turkish Ottoman Empire to the east, and the Austro-Hungarian Habsburg Empire to the west. Vlad spent much of his life fighting both these powers, each of which wanted Wallachia in their empire.

MURDEROUS PRINCE

During his reign, Vlad massacred anyone who got in his way, including women, children, and the infirm. As his nickname suggests, his favourite method of dealing with his enemies was to impale them on blunt wooden stakes. It is said that he killed thousands in this way.

TWO SIDES TO THE TALE

Despite these bloody tales, Vlad is remembered as a national hero in Romania. He defended his territory against the onslaught of foreign powers and, while bloodthirsty, was said to have been a just ruler. During his reign Wallachia was almost crime-free as his subjects knew they would pay a terrible price for any misdemeanours. According to one legend, Vlad left a gold cup by a fountain in a public square. Many used it, but it was never stolen.

WHAT'S IN A NAME?

Vlad's father took the name "Dracul" when he became a member of the Order of the Dragon, whose seal is shown above. Dracula means "son of Dracul", while "Dracul" means dragon or devil in Romanian. Before he came across this striking name, Bram Stoker's villain was destined to be called Count Wampyr.

ELIZABETH Bathory
—THE BLOOD COUNTESS—

In the 1600s, tales emerged of a murderous Hungarian aristocrat. For years Countess Elizabeth Bathory maintained the appearance of normality, while inside her castle she was torturing and murdering scores of innocent girls.

NOBLE BIRTH

Elizabeth Bathory came from one of the richest and most powerful families in the Kingdom of Hungary. She was descended from Transylvanian aristocrats and at the age of 15 married Count Ferenc Nádasdy, a Hungarian military leader. The couple lived in Csejthe Castle in northwest Hungary (in present-day Slovakia). With her husband often away Elizabeth was left to manage the business affairs of the estate.

BLOOD BATH

Legend has it that Elizabeth was a vain woman and used all manner of oils to preserve her skin. One day, the story goes, she hit a servant girl and drew blood, which then dripped onto her skin. As she wiped it away, she thought the skin looked fresher and younger. So it was that the Countess developed her obsession with blood, and concocted a vile scheme to obtain it in huge quantities.

ACCOMPLICES

With the help of a small group of servants – some of whom were said to have links with witchcraft and sorcery – the Countess lured peasant girls from the surrounding countryside to the castle with the promise of work. Once inside, the girls were subject to inhuman torture before being brutally murdered. When the supply of local girls began to run out, Elizabeth offered to teach social graces to young women from noble families. The disappearance of poor servant girls had passed largely unremarked, but when ladies began to go missing, word of the suspicious happenings spread, eventually reaching King Mathias of Hungary.

GRUESOME DISCOVERY

A raid on the castle in late December 1610 uncovered an underground torture chamber, its walls spattered with blood, with bones and other human remains on the ground, along with the clothing and belongings of missing girls. Elizabeth was accused of killing 80 girls, though there was speculation that she was responsible for many more deaths. As a noblewoman, she was never tried for her crimes, though her accomplices were executed. Instead, she was walled up in her bedroom in Csejthe Castle, where she was found dead four years later.

LEGEND

Elizabeth Bathory's crimes are shocking enough, but over the years they have been embellished and turned into gruesome legend. In many retellings the number of victims slaughtered reaches more than 600, and the Countess's sadism is explained as a lust for blood, which she bathes in and even drinks. That this horror story involves a Transylvanian aristocrat has led many people to speculate that Bram Stoker may have read about Elizabeth Bathory and used her story as inspiration for his novel. Though there is no proof of this, there is always a possibility that the character of Dracula was in fact based on a woman.

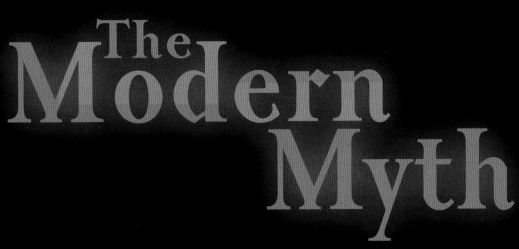

The Modern Myth

Dracula dragged vampires into a new era. They were still deadly, but rather than repulsive they were suave and sophisticated. Since then, vampires have continued to evolve. They are younger, more attractive, and more morally complex. They have gained new powers and can defy many of the old charms and tricks that once kept them at bay. In the fiction of the 21st century, some vampires are battling their very nature to resist the craving for human blood and live side by side with humans.

Horror

Some of the very first horror films ever made were about vampires, and many featured Dracula, or a character based on the famous Count. Since the days of black-and-white movies, screen vampires have changed many times to suit the audience of the day.

DRACULA (1931)
This was the first vampire talkie. Directed by Tod Browning, it starred Bela Lugosi as the Count, whose Hungarian accent, cape, and slicked-back hair became Dracula clichés. Lugosi's Dracula was elegant and debonair, and didn't have fangs.

NOSFERATU (1922)
Considered one of the scariest ever Dracula movies, this German classic was the first film to be based on Bram Stoker's novel. However, the movie was made without the permission of Stoker's estate, so the names of the characters were changed and vampires became "nosferatu". Max Schrek starred as the creepy Count Orlok, who had a grotesque, rat-like appearance and none of Dracula's charm.

VAMPYR (1932)

Based loosely on Sheridan Le Fanu's short story *Carmilla*, Vampyr is a French-German art film telling the story of an old woman revealed to be a vampire in league with the village doctor. She meets her end by being staked with an iron pole.

DRACULA'S DAUGHTER (1936)

The first proper sequel to a Dracula film picks up the story a few moments after *Dracula* ends. Directed by Lambert Hillyer, it features the Count's daughter, who has inherited her father's love of blood.

HOUSE OF DRACULA (1945)

In this American film, Dracula lives with Frankenstein's monster and the Wolfman. Played by John Carradine, Dracula is seeking a cure for his affliction. In a scientific twist, his vampirism is attributed to strange parasites inhabiting his bloodstream.

HORROR OF DRACULA (1958)

Starring Christopher Lee, the first colour version of Stoker's novel took Dracula from castle to bachelor pad and reached a new generation of fans. Lee wore special lenses that turned his eyes red.

DRACULA (1979)

Subtitled "A love story", this adaptation altered much of the plot of the novel to play up the romance. Lucy and Count Dracula have an ill-fated love affair. To make him more believable, Frank Langella's Count had no fangs or coloured contact lenses.

BRAM STROKER'S DRACULA (1992)

In a twist on the original book, Mina falls in love with Dracula, freeing him from his curse so he can die in peace. Gary Oldman's Dracula appears in turn handsome and young, then wizened with age, transforming into a hideous green monster when angry.

Dark Angels
— VAMPIRES COME OF AGE —

Vampires today are almost unrecognizable as the same creatures that featured in so many old Dracula movies. In the 21st century, vampires are no longer the personification of evil — they have evolved into complex beings with hearts, minds, and consciences.

BEAUTIFUL FREAKS

For centuries vampires were predators, pure and simple, but in the late 1970s that changed. Anne Rice's hugely successful *Vampire Chronicles* were the most popular and influential vampire novels since *Dracula*, and they endowed vampirism with positive aspects for the first time. Rice's vampires were deeply sensitive, intellectual, and passionate, with a heightened appreciation of beauty. They had gorgeous, young-looking bodies, and tried to maintain a sense of humanity, despite being compelled to drink blood to stay alive. At the heart of the books is the irrepressible vampire Lestat de Lioncourt. Selfish and arrogant, he loves to make mischief but is not fundamentally evil. Louis de Pointe du Lac, made a vampire by Lestat, despairs at his nature and tries to subsist on the blood of animals.

CONSCIENCE IS KEY

Rice's novels paved the way for a whole new take on the vampire myth. Modern vampires do not fear garlic or whitethorn, they do not run from priests or holy symbols, and their reflections in mirrors prove they are more part of the human world than not. Since they are impervious to sunlight they can lead seemingly normal lives alongside humans, though their ethereal beauty and heightened sensitivity marks them out in the crowd. Most importantly, they have the same spectrum of emotions as humans and are able to make a moral choice about how to live their afterlives. No longer necessarily ruthless creatures driven by appetite, these vampires see their condition as both a curse and a blessing — they revel in their powers but struggle to reconcile their bloodthirsty nature with their human qualities. In the fight of good over evil, it seems that today's vampires can make a choice.

Child Vampires

The idea that a child's innocence could be corrupted by vampirism was once inconceivable. Now, young vampires are everywhere. But whilst some are vicious, others are making friends, tackling bullies, and trying to behave themselves.

LONELINESS

For a child vampire, the innocence of childhood is cut short pretty quickly. As well as being forced by their nature to feed on blood, they have to deal with the realization that while their minds will grow up, their bodies never will. In the movie *Let the Right One In* – based on the novel by John Ajvide Lindqvist – Eli (pictured opposite) is a centuries-old vampire child who lives in a suburb of Stockholm, Sweden. Although Eli has come to terms with being a vampire, she lives an isolated and sad existence. Befriending bullied Oskar, a child who shares her loneliness, she emboldens him to stand up to his tormentors.

TRAPPED

One of the first – and most chilling – child vampires was Claudia in Anne Rice's *Vampire Chronicles*. Claudia has the appearance of a young girl. She makes the most of her child-like appearance and pretends to be frightened and lost. When humans try and help her, she kills them. Claudia has a child's lack of control over her hunger – she kills when she feels like it. Yet in fact she is a woman trapped inside a child's body. Her mind matures, but her body does not. Claudia realizes she will never change, or grow up, yet desperately wants to. For Claudia, this leads to great unhappiness.

TEENAGE ANGST

Not all child vampires are trapped in this way, or behave like brats who can't control their hunger. Many young vampires represent the very opposite – absolute freedom. They have broken free of controlling parents and can look after themselves. These teenage vampires obey no rules but their own, and parents and other authority figures are rarely present. These vampires grow and change, whilst struggling with relationships and their own identity. From Angel, the young vampire in *Buffy the Vampire Slayer*, to Edward Cullen in *Twilight*, they are trying to do the right thing – controlling themselves lest they endanger others.

VAMPIRE *Hunters*

Although these days vampires may have a conscience, those who choose the dark path pose a huge menace. The vampire hunter – or slayer – is our protector in the struggle of good over evil. As vampires have evolved, so too have those who stalk and stake them.

RELUCTANT HERO

Some pursue the undead for religious reasons, others for profit. There are revenge seekers and thrill seekers. Then there are those whose destiny it is to fight vampires whether they like it or not. Buffy Summers, the Chosen One, is one such reluctant hero. First appearing in the 1992 movie *Buffy: The Vampire Slayer*, this hard-fighting teenager went on to feature in the television show of the same name that ran between 1997 and 2003. Defending her hometown of Sunnydale from an onslaught of demonic beasts, Buffy uses the traditional slayer armoury – stakes, sunlight, holy water, decapitation, crucifixes, and fire – as well as some slick street fighting, and is aided by a small band of followers.

BRAINS OVER BRAWN

Before Buffy, the most famous slayer was Abraham Van Helsing, who was pitted against Dracula in Bram Stoker's classic novel. Since then the character has appeared in many reimaginings of Stoker's work, both in print and on screen. Van Helsing represents the vampire hunters who primarily use their intellect, rather than brute strength, to stay one step ahead of their quarry. However, even slayers with innate vampire-fighting capabilities need their wits about them and a knowledge of their prey to succeed.

NEW TRICKS

As vampires have changed, so have their hunters. The weapons that slayers use, for example, have taken on a modern twist. As well as Buffy's high-kicking combat techniques, modern firearms that fire silver bullets, crossbows that launch wooden stakes, and water pistols filled with holy water have become common currency in vampire films. Buffy is an outwardly normal teenager with a secret calling. Other slayers include modern incarnations of the dhampir of Eastern European myth – the hero of the *Blade* series is a half-vampire immune to bites and motivated by the desire for revenge. Now that vampires are more morally complex, so is the relationship between vampire and slayer. No longer always a straightforward fight against evil, today emotions can come into play.

Falling in Love

WITH THE UNDEAD

Vampires in literature have long been figures of fantasy – inspiring a mixture of horror, awe, and fascination. Today's vampire hero is increasingly sympathetic – less murderous villain and more an object of affection, possessing all the powers and instincts of a predator, but with an unmistakably human heart.

TWILIGHT

The vampires in Stephenie Meyer's *Twilight* series have captured the hearts of many readers. The central "family" of vampires – the Cullens – have chosen to drink only animal blood and live in human society. The Cullens' appeal is based on their aloof manner and the air of mystery surrounding them, their artistic accomplishments, and – not least – their astonishing physical beauty. This series of four novels is based on the life of Bella Swan, a teenager who moves to Forks, Washington, and falls in love with the gorgeous Edward Cullen, who happens to be a vampire. He tries to resist his feelings towards Bella, constantly waging war against his baser instincts. While he loves her and doesn't want to harm her, Edward is also deeply attracted to the scent of Bella's blood. He is a 17-year-old who has been alive since 1901 and behaves like an old fashioned gentleman. He opens car doors, pulls out chairs, and defends a girl's honour in front of classroom bullies. What girl could resist?

FORBIDDEN LOVE

Characters like Edward Cullen have transformed the vampire from satanic monster into modern-day hero. This transformation began when a very different take on the vampire appeared. Lestat in *Interview with a Vampire* is one of the boldest and most attractive vampires in fiction.

In Anne Rice's novels he is described as tall, with blond hair and grey eyes that absorb the colours blue or violet from surfaces around them. Lestat is known for being rash, rebellious, and seductive. Characters like Lestat are dangerous, but their menace only adds to their appeal, perhaps because we humans are naturally attracted to things that are forbidden.

INHUMAN HEARTTHROBS

With vampires like these, it's easy to see why humans fall in love with them. They aren't demons hissing at crucifixes, seducing girls and turning them from righteousness to evil. These vampires have a sense of right and wrong – what's more, they can defy death, obliterate their enemies, and stay up all night, all whilst looking impossibly handsome. Their centuries-old eyes gaze out from youthful bodies, fascinating us with their strangeness. They have an air of mystery and power and are capable of deep emotions. Vampires can be especially appealing to those who feel "different", resonating in particular with adolescents, who often feel alienated, misunderstood, and alone. Vampires show very human characteristics – such as neediness, vulnerability, and pride – but have superhuman capabilities. Today, there are many who are happy to accept the vampire's heart as something more than a receptacle for a wooden stake.

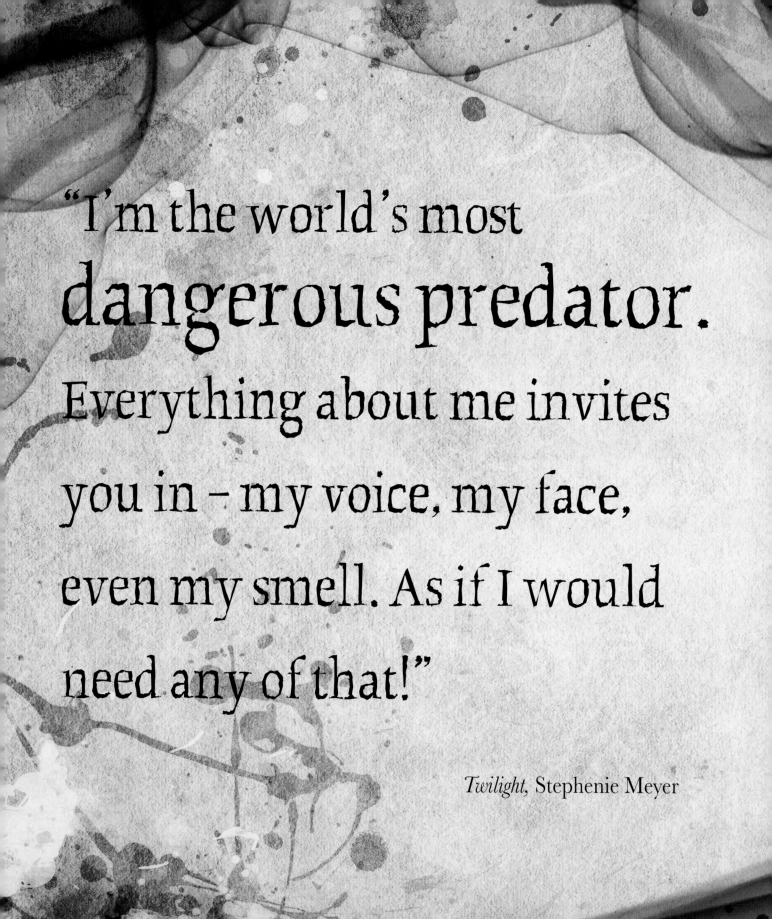

"I'm the world's most dangerous predator. Everything about me invites you in – my voice, my face, even my smell. As if I would need any of that!"

Twilight, Stephenie Meyer

Vampires are **forever**. They change and adapt with each new generation, mirroring the times. Early tales of **revenants**, for example, were often connected to religion and spiritual beliefs. They reflected people's concerns about death and the **afterlife**. Then, with the many advances in science during the 20th century, came scientific explanations for the vampire's condition – it was caused by parasites in the **blood** or was the result of some genetic mutation. Deceptively similar to humans, vampires remain a **race** apart. In some tales, vampires inhabit their own mythic world, which makes little reference to human history. In others, the vampire becomes an entirely separate species, one that has evolved alongside our own. But it is this **difference** that gives vampires their unique appeal and staying power, since it lets us delve into the possibilities, with a **thrill** or two along the way. Vampire stories help us explore our fears surrounding death, **love**, compulsion, and the need to belong. They help us deal with concerns and indulge our fantasies. As long as we have fears and ideas, the vampire will continue to adapt. The vampire's evolution is far from over. . .

More to explore

Fiction

Charnas, Suzy McKee
The Vampire Tapestry, Simon & Schuster, 1980
Vampire Edward Weyland finds himself too involved with the demands of modern society and is forced to hibernate to recover his wild mentality.

Curtis Klause, Annette
The Silver Kiss, Delacorte Press Books for Young Readers, 1990
Zoe is 16 and facing bereavement: her mother is dying of cancer, and her father seems to be excluding her from her mother's hospital bedside. Isolated by fear, Zoe meets the enigmatic Simon, a vampire who has an uncanny ability to recognize her feelings.

Elrod, P N
The Vampire Files, Ace Books, 2003
Investigative journalist Jack Fleming is murdered. He awakens to find himself a vampire and sets about tracking down his killer.

Hahn, Mary Downing
Look for Me by Moonlight, Clarion, 1995
Cynda, staying with her father and his new wife in their supposedly haunted Maine inn, falls in love with a mysterious and handsome guest. But things get difficult when she discovers Victor is a vampire and the murderer of the girl who haunts the inn.

King, Stephen
'Salem's Lot, Doubleday, 1975
'Salem's Lot is short for Jerusalem's Lot, a small town in Maine, New England, where a vampire named Kurt Barlow opens a shop and sucks the blood of the locals, turning them into vampires.

Lindqvist, John Ajvide
Let the Right One In, Quercus Publishing PLC, 2007 (UK)
A new girl called Eli has moved in next door to Oskar. There is something odd about her, and she only comes out at night... Made into an award-winning Swedish film, directed by Tomas Alfredson.

Martin, George R R
Fevre Dream, Poseidon Press, 1982
A good-hearted vampire from Louisiana called Joshua tries to persuade his fellow vampires to change their ways.

Matheson, Richard
I Am Legend, Gollancz, 1954
In this disaster novel, a disease has caused everyone on Earth to become a vampire – except the protagonist, Robert Neville.

Mead, Richelle
Vampire Academy, Puffin, 2007
St Vladimir's Academy is a boarding school where vampires are educated in the ways of magic, and half-human teens train to protect them. Rose Hathaway is a dhampir, a bodyguard for her best friend Lissa, a Moroi Vampire Princess.

Pike, Christopher
The Last Vampire, Hodder Children's Books, 1994
In this six-part series, Alisa Perne is the last vampire. Beautiful and brilliant, she hunts alone, living among humans, sucking their blood. But someone is stalking her and wants her dead.

Rees, Celia
Blood Sinister, Scholastic, 1996
Sixteen-year-old Ellen is dying, and no one knows why. Sent to visit her grandmother, she learns some startling truths when she discovers the diary of her great-grandmother and reads the story of her life, which appears strangely linked to her own.

Rice, Anne
The Vampire Chronicles, Ballantine books, 1976
The most influential vampire novels since Bram Stoker's *Dracula*, in this series the vampire state is described as both a curse and a blessing. Starting with *Interview with the Vampire* (1976), the 10-book series ends with *Blood Canticle* (2003).

Saberhagen, Fred
The Dracula Tape, Warner, 1975
In this response to Bram Stoker's classic, Count Dracula is a good guy who recounts his version of events.

Schreiber, Ellen
Vampire Kisses, Harper Collins Children's Book Group, 2003
Sixteen-year-old Raven, an outcast who always wears black and hopes to become a vampire some day, falls in love with the mysterious new boy in town. She is desperate to find out if he can make her dreams come true.

Shan, Darren
Cirque du Freak, Harper Collins, 2000
A 12-book saga featuring Darren, a young boy who becomes a half-vampire and is apprenticed to an older vampire.

Somtow, S P
Vampire Junction, Donning, 1984
A young vampire, Timmy Valentine, survives the destruction of his town by Mount Vesuvius to become a modern rock star.

Vande Velde, Vivian
Companions of the Night, Jane Yolen Books, 1995
After a late night visit to a laundry, Kerry helps a young boy accused of being a vampire escape from a group of vigilantes; the trouble is, he really does turn out to be one of the undead.

Graphic novels, manga, and anime

Dracula: A Symphony in Moonlight & Nightmares by Jon J Muth (Marvel Graphic Novels, 1986)
Retelling of Dracula as a graphic novel.

Hellsing by Kohta Hirano (Dark Horse Comics, 2003)
In this series the Hellsing Organization defends the world from the onslaught of the powers of darkness.

Chibi Vampire by Tohru Kai, Yuna Kagesaki (TokyoPop, 2003–2008)
Karin Maaka is the middle child of a family of vampires. Karin is very different from the rest of her family. When she bites her "victim", she passes on some of her own blood, leaving both feeling refreshed and energetic. First manga, then novels, and finally anime on Japanese television.

Vampire Hunter D, by Hideyuki Kikuchi, illustrated by Yoshitaka Amano (Dark Horse, 1983–)
This series of Japanese novels feature D, a dhampir, the half-breed child of a vampire father and human mother. The novels led to popular anime and manga.

Blade, by Marv Wolfman, illustrated by Gene Colan (Marvel Comics)
Blade is a vampire hunter, a dhampir. His first appearance was in *The Tomb of Dracula* #10 (July 1973) as a supporting character. Blade went on to star in several comic-book series as well as a television show and film series.

Film

Le Manoir du Diable (1896, Georges Méliès)
Two-minute black-and-white film that is considered the first ever horror movie. It features a bat that transforms itself into a demon, and is killed by a crucifix.

Blood of Dracula (1957, Herbert L Strock)
A student at a school for girls changes into a bloodsucking creature when she falls under a magic spell.

Plan 9 From Outer Space (1959, Edward D Wood)
A silly but fun story about a pair of aliens trying to take over the Earth, with the help of some vampires and corpses.

Love at First Bite (1979, Stan Dragoti)
A vampire spoof. Dracula visits New York City and deals with city life whilst he attempts to find his bride.

Fright Night (1985, Tom Holland)
A teenage horror movie fan becomes convinced that a vampire has moved in next door.

Once Bitten (1985, Howard Storm)
Comic actor Jim Carrey stars as an innocent young man pursued by a seductive female vamp.

The Lost Boys (1987, Joel Schumacher)
After moving to a new town, two brothers are convinced that the area is frequented by vampires. Featuring young vampires and young vampire slayers.

Near Dark (1987, Kathryn Bigelow)
A young man joins a travelling "family" of evil vampires, when he finds out the girl he'd tried to hook up with is part of their group.

Vampire's Kiss (1989, Robert Bierman)
Nicolas Cage plays a New Yorker who thinks he's a vampire. Dark comedy.

Buffy the Vampire Slayer (1992, Fran Rubel Kuzui)
The original movie that spawned the long-running TV series and spin-offs.

Dracula: Dead and Loving it (1995, Mel Brooks)
A spoof of Dracula, starring Leslie Nielsen.

Vampire in Brooklyn (1995, Wes Craven)
Eddie Murphy stars as a vampire from the Caribbean who goes in search of a bride.

Cirque du Freak (2010, Paul Weitz)
A young boy named Darren Shan meets a mysterious man at a freak show who turns out to be a vampire. After a series of events, Darren must leave his normal life and go on the road with the Cirque Du Freak and become a vampire.

Twilight (2008, Catherine Hardwicke)
The film adaptation of the first book in Stephenie Meyer's hugely successful series. Starring Robert Pattinson and Kristen Stewart.

TV

The Night Stalker (John Llewellyn Moxey, Dan Curtis / ABC-TV, USA, 1972)
TV film that was huge in its day. The hero, Carl Kolchak, claims that a vampire is on the loose in Las Vegas. Nobody believes him, so he goes after the vampire himself.

Dark Shadows (Dan Curtis / ABC-TV, USA, 30-min episodes, 1966–1971)
Marathon TV series that ran for 1,225 episodes in the United States, between 1966 and 1971. It features a strange family that included a 175-year-old vampire called Barnabas Collins.

Forever Knight (Nick Knight 1989, CBS, 1992–1995)
The modern-day adventures of an 800-year-old vampire. Nick Knight is a cop who works in Toronto. He tries to make up for his bad bloodsucking ways by fighting crime.

Buffy the Vampire Slayer (Joss Whedon, 1997–2003)
A revamp of the movie, with a more serious side. This long-running series starred Sarah Michelle Geller as the central butt-kicking character.

Being Human (BBC, 2009)
Supernatural drama-comedy series featuring a ghost, a vampire, and a werewolf who share a house in Bristol.

Glossary

Adam
In the Christian Bible, the first man created by God.

apotrope (adj, apotropaic)
Objects, such as amulets and talismans, that are displayed to ward off evil.

aristocrat
Someone born into the aristocracy (the ruling class).

art film
An independent movie intended to be considered for its artistic worth, rather than its commercial value.

asafoetida
A dried gum that comes from the giant fennel plant. It has a very pungent garlic smell when raw.

Attila the Hun
The emperor of the Huns (a people based in modern-day Hungary) from 434 to 453 CE. Attila was a fierce warrior, with a reputation for cruelty.

Aztecs
A people from central Mexico of the 14th, 15th, and 16th centuries, who practised human sacrifice.

Banshee
A fairy of Irish mythology who wails to foretell the deaths of great men.

Black Death
Outbreak of bubonic plague that killed millions around the world in the mid-14th century. Bubonic plague is a deadly disease caused by the bacteria *Yersinia pestis*, that results in black swellings in the armpits and groin, and is passed to humans by the fleas that live on infected rats.

caul
A thin, filmy membrane that sometimes covers a baby when it is born.

corpse
A dead body.

crucifix
An ancient symbol of Jesus on the cross. It shows the death of Jesus by crucifixion, and is said to scare off vampires.

dark gift
A term used in Anne Rice's *Vampire Chronicles* to describe the condition of being a vampire.

deity
A god or goddess.

demon
An evil spirit or monster.

fairy
A mythical creature often taking human form, described as having magic powers.

fangs
Long pointed canine teeth, used for biting and tearing. In vampires, the fangs are the upper canines, used for piercing the skin of victims to allow their blood to be sucked out.

folklore
The collection of popular tales and beliefs, often passed on through word of mouth, that reflect the history or culture of a group of people.

Garden of Eden
In the Bible, the place where the first man and woman, Adam and Eve, lived.

garlic
A bulb-like plant related to the onion.

Gothic
An elaborate architectural style that flourished during the Middle Ages, used in many castles of that period. The style was revived in the late 18th century and gave its name to a genre of English fiction that featured tales of mystery or horror in a dark and macabre setting.

Habsburg Empire
The empire of the powerful Habsburg dynasty, a ruling house of Europe. First established in the 13th century, at its peak it controlled the modern-day countries of Austria, Hungary, Czech Republic, Slovakia, Slovenia, Croatia, and parts of many others.

Hebrew
The Jewish Holy Language, dating from around the 6th century BCE.

hypnotic
Relating to hypnosis – when someone's words or actions make you fall into a trance so that you follow their suggestions and commands.

immigrant
Someone who is new to a country or area and chooses to settle there permanently.

immortal
Living in a spiritual or physical form for all time.

Kingdom of Hungary
A state in central Europe that was established around 1000 and included Hungary as well as part of modern-day Romania, Ukraine, and Croatia.

legend
A story from the past, sometimes one popularly supposed to have a historical basis but which is not verifiable.

Maya
A civilization of Mexico and Central America that existed until conquered by the Spanish in the early 16th century.

Mesopotamia
This region of southwest Asia between the Tigris and Euphrates rivers is now in modern Iraq and Syria. Considered the cradle of civilization, it was home to some of the world's earliest civilizations.

myth
A traditional story, often involving the supernatural.

mythical
Existing only in myths and folk tales.

occult
Involving magic and the paranormal.

Ottoman Empire
Also known as the Turkish Empire, this was a vast empire that existed between the 13th and 20th centuries. At its height it spanned three continents, including much of southeastern Europe, the Middle East, and North Africa.

predator
Something that hunts, then feeds on, its prey.

principality
A state ruled by a prince.

regenerative
Able to heal and replace lost or damaged tissues – to heal wounds and grow back organs and limbs.

resurrection
Coming to life again; returning from the dead.

revenant
A person that has returned from the dead, including ghosts, zombies, and vampires. Term used especially in Medieval Europe to refer to the undead.

Rhode Island
The smallest state in New England, USA.

shape shift
The ability to transform from one physical form into another.

Shiva
Hindu god of destruction.

sorcerer
Someone who practises magic.

species
A particular kind of animal or plant. Members of the same species share common characteristics.

stake
A wooden stick with a sharp point.

Summers, Montague (1880–1948)
Famous vampire expert who wrote exhaustively on the subject.

supernatural
Things that occur or exist beyond the realms of scientific understanding.

talkie
A motion picture with a synchronized soundtrack. The first films were silent – there was no technology available to hear what the actors were saying.

tam-o'-shanter
A Scottish bonnet worn by men, named after a character from a famous poem by Robert Burns. It is made of tartan wool with a bobble in the middle.

Transylvania
A part of modern-day Romania, encompassing the Carpathian Mountains.

tuberculosis
Often shortened to TB, this infectious disease used to be very common and was frequently fatal. It attacks the lungs, and symptoms include a fever, night sweats, bloody phlegm, and weight loss.

quarry
A person or animal that is being hunted.

undead
Beings that are technically dead, but behave as if they are alive.

vampire bat
Bats, native to South America, whose food source is blood. They are active at night, and will sometimes attack sleeping humans.

Voodoo
A religion practised in Haiti and the southern United States, combining the spiritual beliefs of West African peoples with Roman Catholicism.

Wallachia
A principality situated to the south of the Carpathian Mountains, now a part of Romania. It lasted from the 14th to the 19th century.

zombie
A dead person who is brought back to life as a reanimated corpse or mindless being by voodoo sorcerers, traditionally from West Africa and Haiti.

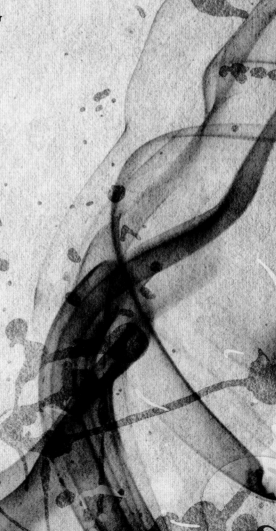

Index

Credits

DK would like to thank:
Steven Carton, Ashwin Khurana, and Niki Foreman for editorial assistance; Scarlett O'Hara for proofreading; Jackie Brind for the index; Stefan Podhorodecki for photography; Neil Amon, Jade Cresswell (MOT-models), Glenn Walker, and Rosie Williams for modelling; Valero Doval, Illustration Ltd., Francesco Francavilla, KJA-Artists.com, and Katie Knutton for illustrations.

The publisher would like to thank the following for their kind permission to reproduce their photographs:

Key:
a-above; b-below/bottom; c-centre; f-far; l-left; r-right; t-top

5 **iStockphoto.com:** Aleksandar Velasevic (cb). 6 **Dreamstime.com:** Devor (bl). 7 **Dreamstime.com:** Devor (br) (tl); Halilo (c). 8–9 **iStockphoto.com:** Nocturnus (c). 10–11 **iStockphoto.com:** mxtama (c). 12–13 **iStockphoto.com:** goktugg (c/splashed background); proxyminder (c/blue smoke effect). 18 **Corbis:** Images.com (tl) (bl) (tr). 19 **Corbis:** Images.com (br) (bl) (tl) (tr). 20–21 **Corbis:** Ron Nickel / Design Pics (c/woman boarding bus). 21 **Corbis:** W. Perry Conway (br). 22 **Alamy Images:** WoodyStock (ca/bats). **Getty Images:** CGIBackgrounds.com (c). 26–27 **iStockphoto.com:** duncan1890 (c/abstract background); sbayram (c/water). 30 **iStockphoto.com:** red_frog (cl). 30–31 **iStockphoto.com:** Phecs (c/background). 32–33 **iStockphoto.com:** guysargent (c/stone wall). 34–35 **Getty Images:** Dorling Kindersley (c/tree bark). 38 **Dreamstime.com:** Kizkulesi (tl) (bl). 38–39 **Alamy Images:** Ian Dagnall (cl/sunset scene). 39 **Alamy Images:** jean (tr). 40 **Corbis:** Phillipe Lissac (c). 42–43 Chris Hope: hopedraws.com (c). 46–47 **Corbis:** Barry Lewis (tc/fire ball). **iStockphoto.com:** kjohansen (cl/textured background). 47 **iStockphoto.com:** provrb7 (ca/shutters). 48–49 **Alamy Images:** Images Etc Ltd (tc/sky). 50–51 **iStockphoto.com:** Angel_1978 (c/ornate border); bphillips (c/decaying background); Aleksandar Velasevic (c/wings). 52–53 **The Bridgeman Art Library:** Maison de Victor Hugo, Paris, France / Lauros / Giraudon (c). 55 **Corbis:** Benelux / zefa (ca). 58–59 **Corbis:** Luke MacGregor. 60 Ronald Correia: (c). **Dreamstime.com:** Alptraum (br/rose). 61 **Ronald Correia:** (crb). 62 **British Library:** (fbl). **Corbis:** moodboard (c). **TopFoto.co.uk:** Fortean (bc). 62–63 **iStockphoto.com:** bphillips (c/background). 63 **Dreamstime.com:** Elise1976 (cra/design behind bat). 64 **Dreamstime.com:** Angie68 (tl) (tr). 66–67 **iStockphoto.com:** benoitb (c/water drops); Cloudniners (c/scrolls). 68–69 **Alamy Images:** Chris Howes/Wild Places Photography (c/forest scene). 69 **Alamy Images:** Melvyn Longhurst (clb). 72–73 **iStockphoto.com:** wragg (c). 74 **Getty Images:** John Lund (c/darkroom). **The Kobal Collection:** Universal (tr). **Rex Features:** Everett Collection (bl). 74–75 **Dreamstime.com:** Bogalo (cr/film strips). 75 **Alamy Images:** Photos 12 (bc). **The Kobal Collection:** Dreyer-Tobis-Klangfilm (tl); Universal (tr) (bl). **The Ronald Grant Archive:** American Zoetrope / RGA (br); **Universal Pictures** (tc). 76 **iStockphoto.com:** Yuri_Arcurs (ca). 76–77 **Alamy Images:** les polders (c). 78–79 **The Kobal Collection:** Fido Film AB (c). 81 **The Kobal Collection:** 20th Century Fox TV/Richard Cartwright (c). 82 **iStockphoto.com:** Cloudniners (bl/scroll). **The Kobal Collection:** Maverick Films (c). 83 **Getty Images:** Ryan McVay (c/background trees). **iStockphoto.com:** Cloudniners (tr/scroll). 84–85 **iStockphoto.com:** goktugg (c/splashes); proxyminder (c/smoke).

Jacket images:

Front: photography by Andy Crawford. **iStockphoto.com:** Aleksandar Velasevic c (wings). Back: **iStockphoto.com:** Aleksandar Velasevic (c/trees); **NASA:** (c/moon); Front endpapers: **iStockphoto.com:** Natouche (c/roses); Snaprender (c/coffins); **Rex Features:** Peter Brooker (crb/open coffin). Back endpapers: **iStockphoto.com:** Natouche (c/roses); Snaprender (c/coffins); **Rex Features:** Peter Brooker (crb/open coffin).

All other images © Dorling Kindersley

For further information see:

www.dkimages.com